Treasure Hunt

Read more Animal Inn books!

BOOK 1: A Furry Fiasco

Coming soon:

BOOK 3: The Bow-wow Bus

ANIMAL INN
Treasure Hunt

Book 2

PAUL DUBOIS JACOBS
&
JENNIFER SWENDER

Illustrated by STEPHANIE LABERIS

ALADDIN

New York   London   Toronto   Sydney   New Delhi

This book is a work of fiction. Any references to historical events, real people, or real places are used fictitiously. Other names, characters, places, and events are products of the author's imagination, and any resemblance to actual events or places or persons, living or dead, is entirely coincidental.

ALADDIN

An imprint of Simon & Schuster Children's Publishing Division

1230 Avenue of the Americas, New York, New York 10020

First Aladdin paperback edition December 2016

Text copyright © 2016 by Simon & Schuster, Inc.

Illustrations copyright © 2016 by Stephanie Laberis

Also available in an Aladdin hardcover edition.

All rights reserved, including the right of reproduction in whole or in part in any form.

ALADDIN and related logo are registered trademarks of Simon & Schuster, Inc.

For information about special discounts for bulk purchases, please contact Simon & Schuster Special Sales at 1-866-506-1949 or business@simonandschuster.com.

The Simon & Schuster Speakers Bureau can bring authors to your live event. For more information or to book an event, contact the Simon & Schuster Speakers Bureau at 1-866-248-3049 or visit our website at www.simonspeakers.com.

Cover designed by Jessica Handelman

Interior designed by Greg Stadnyk

The illustrations for this book were rendered digitally.

The text of this book was set in Bembo Std.

Manufactured in the United States of America 1116 OFF

2 4 6 8 10 9 7 5 3 1

Library of Congress Control Number 2016936119

ISBN 978-1-4814-6227-3 (hc)

ISBN 978-1-4814-6226-6 (pbk)

ISBN 978-1-4814-6228-0 (eBook)

For Mary Anne A.

PROLOGUE

Ring-ring!

Ring-ring!

Our phone is always ringing.

Ring-ring!

Welcome to Animal Inn. My name is Dash. I'm a Tibetan terrier.

No, I'm not from Tibet. I live in the Virginia countryside. To be honest, I'm not even a terrier.

When people outside of Tibet first saw my ancestors, they thought we looked like terriers.

We Tibetan terriers are shaggy and surefooted. We're known as good luck charms and as excellent companions. This comes in handy because I am a companion to *a lot* of animals and people.

I live with my family, the Tylers—Mom, Dad, Jake, Ethan, and Cassie—plus six other pets:

- Leopold—a scarlet macaw
- Coco—a chocolate Labrador retriever
- Shadow and Whiskers—sister and brother cats
- and Fuzzy and Furry—a pair of very adventurous gerbils

We used to live in an apartment in the city. But when kid number three and dog number two joined the family, Mom and Dad bought this old house in the country.

Animal Inn is one part hotel, one part school, and one part spa. As our brochure says: *We promise to love your pet as much as you do.*

Ring-ring!

Would someone please answer the phone?

It could be a Pekinese for a pedicure. A Siamese for a short stay. Or a llama for a long stay. We even had a Komodo dragon bunk in our basement. But that's another story. It's no wonder the phone is always ringing.

On the first floor of Animal Inn, we have the Welcome Area, the office, the classroom, the party and play room, and the grooming room.

Our family lives on the second floor. This includes Fuzzy and Furry locked in their gerbiltorium in Jake and Ethan's room. (More about this later.)

The third floor is for smaller animals. Any guest who needs an aquarium, a terrarium, or a solarium stays on the third floor.

Ring-ring!

Where is everybody?

I know I have excellent hearing, but am I the only one who hears the phone? Maybe everyone else is out in the barn and kennels. That's where the larger animals stay.

Here at Animal Inn we pride ourselves on calm and comfort. But that was put to the test when we were almost raided by pirates.

Let me tell you what happened. . . .

CHAPTER
1

The day began like any other

Saturday morning.

When I padded downstairs, the sun was just coming up. Mom was already in the Welcome Area with a cup of coffee in one hand and a to-do list in the other.

Leopold was on his perch, his feathers neatly groomed. Leopold always likes to look his best.

"Good morning, Leopold," I said. "Nice day, isn't it?"

"Yes," Leopold agreed. "Nice and quiet."

Dad soon came downstairs with an armload of camping equipment.

"Did you find the poles?" Mom asked him.

Dad held up the tent poles. "Got 'em," he answered. "Are you sure you can manage here alone?"

"I'll be fine," Mom said, checking her to-do list. "It's going to be a quiet day."

I looked at Leopold. Leopold looked at me. Saturdays at Animal Inn are rarely quiet.

In fact, Saturday is our busiest day. Mom teaches her Polite Puppies class. Dad and Jake host the Furry Pages. That's when children read aloud to an animal buddy. Then there are grooming

Welcome!

Please Ring Bell!

appointments and usually a birthday party or two.

"I've got it all worked out," Mom began. "Polite Puppies are going to join Furry Pages. That way I can run both programs at the same time. Plus, Mary Anne from the library is coming to give me a hand."

"Sounds like a great plan," said Dad.

My ears perked up. I love when Mary Anne comes to Furry Pages. She always brings cool books from the library.

"We have only one grooming appointment," Mom continued. "Monsieur Petit. Martha will do that. There are no parties, and we're not expecting any new guests."

"You're right," Dad said with a smile. "A quiet day."

I let out a sigh. We needed a quiet day.

The day before, we had said good-bye to 2,311 monarch butterflies. They had been spending a few days at our milkweed patch on their way to Mexico. During the previous few weeks waves of monarchs had been stopping at Animal Inn to relax and recharge.

Suddenly I heard Ethan from upstairs. "Where's *my* sleeping bag?" he hollered.

"I don't know," shouted Jake. "Did you put it in the pile?"

"Where's the pile?" Ethan asked.

"Yeah," chirped Cassie. "Where's the Nile? Is that where we're camping tonight?"

"We're not camping on the Nile," said Ethan. "The Nile is in Africa."

"Ethan!" Jake shouted. "Did you feed Fuzzy and Furry?"

"I thought you fed them!" Ethan shouted back.

Mom looked at Dad. "Are you sure *you're* going to be okay?"

Dad smiled and shrugged. Then he hurried upstairs to help the kids.

A few minutes later Cassie and Coco came downstairs. Shadow followed in their . . . shadow. Shadow is supposed to be an indoor cat, but she loves to sneak outside.

"Don't tell anybody I'm here," Shadow whispered to Leopold and me. She snuck behind the sofa, ready to slip outside if given the chance.

"Princess Coco," Cassie said, pouting. "The campground says no dogs allowed. They're meanies."

"Good morning, Cassie," said Mom. "Are you excited to go camping?"

"Sort of," said Cassie. "I wish Coco could come. Maybe I can dress her up like a person." Cassie took off her jacket and tried to put it on Coco. Coco gave a big shake.

"Coco can help me with Polite Puppies and Furry Pages," Mom said. "Then she and I can take a nice, long afternoon nap." Coco flopped down onto the floor with a sigh.

Dad, Jake, and Ethan came downstairs next. It was difficult to see them through the jumble of camping supplies they carried.

"Better late than never," Leopold squawked.

"Very funny, Leopold," said Ethan.

"Are you sure you'll be able to manage here alone?" Dad asked Mom again.

"Alone?" said Mom with a smile. "I've got Dash, Leopold, Coco, Shadow, and Whiskers."

"And Fuzzy and Furry," added Ethan.

"And don't forget the guests," said Jake. "You've got four frogs, a turtle, and two hamsters on the third floor, an alpaca in the barn, and a cat and three dogs in the kennel."

I had to agree. You're never really alone at Animal Inn.

CHAPTER 2

Loading the car was a bit hectic,
but the campers finally left. The Welcome Area
was quiet again.

"Ah," sighed Mom. She sat down on the sofa.
"A whole weekend to myself."

"Leopold is a pretty bird," Leopold squawked.

"You're right," Mom said with a smile. "I

couldn't forget you, Leopold. Or you, Dash." She gave me a pat on the head.

"There is one thing I need to do," said Mom. "I need to e-mail a coupon to our mailing list—five percent off any Animal Inn service. After that, it's Polite Puppies and Furry Pages, a few chores, and then we can all relax." She stood up and headed for the office.

Maybe this would be a calm Saturday after all. Coco was already asleep on the floor, softly snoring.

"Wow," came a voice from the bottom of the stairs. "It's so peaceful down here today."

It was Whiskers. Whiskers tends to be a little nervous. He made his way across the Welcome Area and happily settled into his usual spot on the sofa.

Ding-dong!

"Who could that be?" asked Mom, coming out of the office. She hurried to answer the front door.

It was Cassie. She looked like she was going to cry.

"What's wrong?" asked Mom. "Did you forget something?"

"I miss Coco," Cassie said with a sniffle. Coco sleepily raised her head.

Mom leaned down and wiped away Cassie's first tears. "It's only for one night, sweetheart," she said.

"I know," said Cassie. "But I want to stay home."

Dad soon followed. He held Cassie's gear under one arm, and Shadow under the other. He shrugged. "One wants to abandon ship. One wants to stow away."

Mom smiled and took Shadow from Dad.

Dad put down Cassie's gear. "Try as I might, I couldn't change her mind," he said.

"It's fine," said Mom. "Cassie can help me here."

Cassie ran over and gave Coco a big hug.

"I guess we'll see you tomorrow," said Dad.

Mom kissed Dad good-bye, put Shadow down, and went back to the office. Cassie stayed glued to Coco.

"Good try," I whispered to Shadow.

Shadow huffed. "I sneezed in the car and gave myself away."

"Well, I'm glad you're back," said Whiskers. "We're going to have a quiet day."

"You mean a *boring* day," scoffed Shadow.

Ring-ring!

Ring-ring!

"Hello. Animal Inn," we heard Mom say from the office. "I'm having trouble hearing you. Can you speak louder? You're at the harbor?"

Whiskers looked up from the sofa.

"Today?" we heard Mom ask. "It is a bit last-minute. What's the guest's name?"

"A new guest?" said Cassie, perking up. She hurried toward the office door. Coco started to follow her.

"Sorry, Coco," Cassie said. "You know the rules. No animals allowed in the office."

Coco flopped back down onto the floor with a sigh.

"The name is Blackbeard?" we heard Mom ask.

"Blackbeard?" Cassie said excitedly. "That sounds like a pirate name." She disappeared into the office.

"Did Cassie just say 'pirate'?" Whiskers asked with a worried look.

"I believe so," said Leopold.

"Awesome!" said Shadow. "Pirates are way cooler than Polite Puppies."

CHAPTER
3

"Hold on," I said. "Let's not get

ahead of ourselves. Remember what happened
with Miss KD?"

Miss KD was the Komodo dragon who stayed
in our basement. Before her arrival, there were a
lot of misunderstandings about what she was.

"First we thought she was a wizard," I reminded

Whiskers. "Then we thought she was a real, fire-breathing dragon."

"In the end," said Leopold, "she was a polite guest and a good friend. And we learned not to believe everything Cassie says."

"It's not just what Cassie said," insisted Whiskers. "It's what Mom said. Harbor? Blackbeard? It can mean only one thing."

"A pirate!" cheered Shadow. "To think, a real plank-walking, treasure-seeking, sword-wielding pirate is coming here to Animal Inn."

We actually knew a lot about pirates. Pirate stories were a favorite choice for family movies and Furry Pages.

"Don't pirates have crews?" Whiskers asked worriedly. "What if *lots* of pirates are coming?"

"The more salty dogs the better," said Shadow.

"Salty dogs?" asked Coco, suddenly awake. "Do you eat them with ketchup? Or mustard?"

"Salty dogs are not something to eat," I explained.

"Salty dogs are pirates," said Leopold.

"Pirates?" asked Coco. "Why are we talking about pirates?"

"Haven't you been listening?" Whiskers asked.

"No," said Coco. "I've been napping. I thought we were having a quiet day."

"A last-minute guest is coming," I explained. "The name is Blackbeard."

Ding-dong!

"Batten down the hatches!" Whiskers screeched.

"Shiver me timbers," Shadow said with a grin. She snuck back behind the sofa.

Mom and Cassie came out from the office to answer the door. I pointed with my nose to alert Mom that, yes, Shadow was hiding behind the sofa.

"Thank you, Dash," she said.

To our surprise it really was . . .

Not a pirate.

It was Mary Anne, the librarian.

"Come on in," said Mom, holding open the door.

"Good morning. I brought books for Furry Pages," said Mary Anne. She held out a big bag of books. "Cassie, do you want to help me choose some favorites?"

"Yes," said Cassie. "Can Coco help too?"

"Of course," said Mary Anne.

"I'll join you in a minute," said Mom. "I need to get ready for a last-minute guest."

"It's a harbor pirate," Cassie told Mary Anne.

Mary Anne smiled. "That's exciting," she said.

Cassie and Mary Anne headed to the classroom. Coco followed close behind.

"*See?*" said Whiskers. "It *is* a pirate." He buried

his head under a sofa cushion. "I don't want to walk the plank. All I want is a quiet day."

"It will be a quiet day," I said.

I hoped I was right.

CHAPTER
4

"**Good morning, everyone,**" Mary Anne announced. "Welcome to Furry Pages and Polite Puppies."

As Cassie and Mary Anne handed out books to the children, the puppies tugged and pulled on the carpet squares. The puppies were still learning to be polite.

I had a moment to think. *Why would a pirate*

come to Animal Inn? I couldn't think of any logical reason. Surely we had nothing to worry about.

Cassie brought Coco over to my carpet square so that she could read to both of us.

"I found a pirate book!" she said excitedly. She held up *Eloise's Pirate Adventure*.

It's only a book, I told myself.

Cassie started reading. Soon I could hear Coco softly snoring. Well, I guess that *is* the sign of a good bedtime story.

Mom hurried into the classroom. "Sorry I'm late," she said. She had the phone in one hand and her to-do list in the other.

While the kids read, the parents chatted quietly. Mary Anne passed out puppy snacks, and people snacks too. She and Mom helped the children sound out difficult words.

Soon most of the puppies were snoozing just like Coco. Maybe it would be a quiet day after all.

Ring-ring!

Ring-ring!

"Animal Inn," Mom answered. "Oh, hi again. Yes, we do have parrot food."

Parrot food? I thought.

"Of course," Mom said. "There's plenty of space for Blackbeard to dig."

Did she just say "dig"?

"Can you e-mail me the information?" Mom asked. "I'm sure we'll find a safe place for your treasure."

Treasure!

A pirate is dangerous enough. But a pirate with treasure to hide? Maybe we did have something to worry about after all.

How could Mom be so calm? Wasn't she nervous about the new guest? I hurried to the Welcome Area.

"Leopold," I whispered. "We may have a real problem." I filled him in on what I'd just heard.

"We're going to need assistance," said Leopold. "Follow me to the gerbiltorium."

We rushed up the stairs to Jake and Ethan's room. Fuzzy and Furry were lounging in one of their play structures.

"Hi, Dash. Hi, Leopold," said Fuzzy.

"Care for a snack?" added Furry. He held out a sunflower seed.

"No time," I said. "We need your help."

"It involves computers," said Leopold.

"No problem," said Fuzzy. "You've heard of a computer mouse?"

"We're computer gerbils," added Furry.

"We're very tech-savvy," said Fuzzy.

"But it will cost you," added Furry.

"How many dog biscuits?" I asked.

"Not dog biscuits," said Fuzzy.

"We're talking walnuts," added Furry.

"I can get walnuts," said Leopold.

"Deal," said Fuzzy.

"Give us the details," added Furry.

"We need information about a last-minute guest," I explained. "Your job is to sneak into the office and print out an e-mail."

"Easy," said Fuzzy. "Is the e-mail coming to Mom's address or to Dad's address?"

"Or the general Animal Inn address?" added Furry.

"We don't know," I said. "But look for any message with the word 'Blackbeard' or 'treasure.'"

"Did you say '*treasure*'?" asked Fuzzy.

"We are expert treasure-hunters," added Furry.

"We have quite a collection," said Fuzzy.

"We keep it locked in the old chest in the attic," added Furry.

"We recently added a windup mouse and a rubber hot dog," said Fuzzy.

"Would you like to see them?" added Furry.

"Maybe later," I said. "But right now we need that e-mail."

"It's extremely urgent," said Leopold.

"No sweat," said Fuzzy.

"We know all the passwords," added Furry.

They giggled and picked the lock on the gerbiltorium. Then they scampered into the heating vent and disappeared.

CHAPTER 5

Leopold and I rushed back downstairs.

Yip! Yip! Yap! Yap! Yap!

The dismissal of Furry Pages and Polite Puppies was a bit chaotic.

Yap! Yap!

Owners were chasing after puppies. Tail-wagging puppies were chasing after one another.

Mary Anne did her best to hand bookmarks out to the children.

As Mom and Cassie waved good-bye to the last puppy, a few leaves blew into the Welcome Area.

"That was quite a whirlwind," said Mom, shutting the door. Then she, Cassie, and Mary Anne went back to the classroom to clean up. Polite Puppies can make quite a mess.

"All clear," Leopold said from his perch. I nodded and took my position at the office door.

"What's going on?" Whiskers asked from the sofa.

"Fuzzy and Furry are getting information about the last-minute guest," whispered Leopold.

"They're in the office now," I added.

"But I thought there was nothing to worry about," Whiskers said.

"That's what we're trying to find out," I answered.

I listened carefully, my ear to the door. I heard noises coming from inside the office—shuffling and clicking and beeping noises.

"What's Mom's password?" I heard Fuzzy ask.

"Dash–Tibetan–seven," said Furry.

I stood up a little straighter. I hadn't known I was Mom's password.

"Nothing there," said Fuzzy. "What's Dad's?"

"Leopold–macaw–eight," said Furry.

"Nothing there," said Fuzzy. "What about the general Animal Inn address?"

"*J-E-C*-three-*S-W*-two-*F-F*-two," said Furry.

"How do you remember all that?" asked Fuzzy.

"Easy," said Furry. "*J* is for Jake. *E* is for Ethan. *C* is for Cassie. The number three is for three kids. *S* is for Shadow. *W* is for Whiskers. Two is for . . ."

Suddenly I noticed Leopold. He was waving a wing to get my attention.

I quickly stepped away from the office door.

Mom and Mary Anne were coming back into the Welcome Area. Cassie and Coco followed.

"Thanks so much for your help today," said Mom.

"I had a lot of fun," said Mary Anne, waving good-bye.

Mom shut the front door and took out her to-do list. Her next stop would probably be the office.

I looked at Leopold. Leopold looked at me and nodded.

Squawk! Squawk!

Squawk! Squawk!

Hopefully, his squawks sent a clear message to Fuzzy and Furry: *Hurry up!*

I inched closer to the office door. I heard a few more beeps and clicks.

"Say cheese!" said Fuzzy.

"Smile!" added Furry.

I heard a whir, a rip, a double-thump, and a skitter.

"Is it time for lunch yet?" Cassie asked. She flopped onto the floor next to Coco.

"Almost," said Mom. "I just need to e-mail that coupon for five percent off."

I gulped. I sure hoped Fuzzy and Furry were finished.

Ding-dong!

"Now, who could that be?" said Mom.

Whew! I thought. Saved by the bell.

Mom opened the front door. It was Mary Anne with Shadow under one arm.

"I found this stowaway in the back of my pickup truck," Mary Anne said with a smile.

"Sorry about that," said Mom. She took Shadow from Mary Anne. "Twice in one day, Shadow?" she asked, setting her down on the floor. Shadow quickly scampered behind the sofa.

"*Now* is it time for lunch?" asked Cassie.

Mom nodded. "Just need to send the e-mail."

Cassie followed Mom into the office. I held my breath.

"That's odd," I heard Mom say. "I don't remember sending the coupon. But I guess I did. It says right here, 'Message sent.'"

I looked at Leopold. Leopold looked at me.

What had Fuzzy and Furry done now?

CHAPTER
6

Fuzzy and Furry poked their heads out of the heating vent in the Welcome Area. They looked a little bleary-eyed from staring at the computer.

"Thanks for the squawk, Leopold," said Fuzzy.

"We got away just in time," added Furry.

"What did you find?" I asked.

"First," said Fuzzy, "the new computer is awesome."

"It can play music, take pictures, and even show movies," added Furry.

"Second, we found a box of paper clips," said Fuzzy.

"Good for picking locks," added Furry.

"Third, there are new photos on the wall," said Fuzzy.

"There's a nice one of you and Leopold," added Furry.

"And another of Shadow and Whiskers," said Fuzzy.

"And one of Coco eating cheese," added Furry.

"Did someone say 'cheese'?" Coco asked, opening her eyes.

"But there's no picture of us," sighed Furry.

This was typical of the gerbils. They were easily distracted.

"Guys," I interrupted. "Did you find the e-mail?"

"Oh, we found the e-mail," said Fuzzy.

"We printed it out," added Furry.

"First the paper jammed," said Fuzzy.

"Then it unjammed," added Furry.

"So, where is it?" asked Leopold.

"We have it right here," said Fuzzy. He pulled a crumpled piece of paper out of the heating vent.

"But we didn't have time to read it," added Furry.

"I can read it for you," offered Coco.

"Hang on just a second," said Shadow. She strolled out from behind the sofa. "*You* can read, Coco? When did you learn?"

"Furry Pages," said Coco. "You should join us sometime. It's very educational. I started with

Go, Dog. Go! But you might want to try *The Cat in the Hat.*"

Coco took the paper from Fuzzy. She smoothed it out on the floor with her paws.

"It says, 'Overnight delivery *cone*-formation.'" Coco looked up. "What is a *cone*-formation? Is it like an ice-cream cone?"

I looked at the page. I said, "It's not '*cone*-formation.' It's '*confirmation.*' Overnight delivery confirmation."

"What about Blackbeard?" Whiskers asked nervously.

"What about the treasure?" asked Shadow.

I looked at the page more carefully. It had nothing to do with pirates. "This is an e-mail receipt," I said. "It's from a company called Picture *Purr*fect."

"Uh-oh," said Fuzzy. "We may have printed the wrong e-mail."

"We were in a rush," added Furry.

"What now?" asked Whiskers.

I thought for a moment. "As a precaution," I said, "we should have a lookout."

"We can be the lookout," said Fuzzy.

"We're expert lookouts," added Furry.

"To the crow's nest!" said Fuzzy.

"It's a *real* crow's nest," added Furry. They scampered off into the heating vent.

"I can't wait to see the Jolly Roger," said Shadow.

"Jolly?" asked Whiskers. "That doesn't sound scary. And who's Roger?"

"The 'Jolly Roger' is another name for the pirate flag," explained Leopold. "It traditionally features a skull and crossbones."

Whiskers's fur stood on end. "Skulls and bones!" he cried.

"Stay calm," I said. "Let's think. What do we know for certain?"

"We know someone named Blackbeard is coming," said Leopold.

"We know he's coming from the harbor," added Coco.

"We know he has a treasure," said Shadow.

"And we also know pirates carry swords!" cried Whiskers.

"Swords-shmords," said Shadow. "I can't wait to get my paws on that treasure chest. I bet it's filled with gold doubloons or precious jewels. We are going to be rich!"

"Maybe the treasure chest is filled with cheese," said Coco.

"Cheese?" scoffed Shadow.

"Sure," said Coco. "Grilled cheese or mac-and-cheese or just plain cheese. A whole treasure chest full of cheese. Yum."

"Whatever the treasure turns out to be," said Leopold, "we should hand it over to Mom and Dad. They'll know what to do with it."

"They should use it to buy a security system," whimpered Whiskers, "to protect us against pirate raids."

"Or," said Coco, "they could buy more cheese."

CHAPTER
7

Ring-ring!

Ring-ring!

Mom hurried into the Welcome Area from the office. Cassie followed her.

"Where did I leave that phone?" Mom said. She dug around the sofa cushions. "Whiskers, have you seen the phone?"

Ring-ring!

"Sounds like it's in the classroom," said Mom. She hurried off to find it.

"Hi, Coco," said Cassie, coming over and giving her a big hug. "It's almost time for lunch." Coco sighed happily.

Mom came back to the Welcome Area with the phone to her ear. "Sounds good. We'll see you Thursday for Fritz's grooming appointment. You'd like to use the e-mail coupon? Great."

Then she suddenly stopped.

"Wait . . . *fifty* percent off? Are you sure it doesn't say *five* percent off? Okay, then. We'll see you on Thursday."

Mom hung up the phone. "That's odd," she said. "I know I wrote 'five percent off.' And no one else has been on the computer today."

I looked at Leopold. Leopold looked at me.

Mom didn't know it, but someone else had been on her computer. *Two* someones to be exact.

"Is it time for lunch yet?" asked Cassie. "Look at poor Coco. She's so hungry."

"Tell you what," said Mom. "Let's take the dogs for a walk. We'll check on the guests in the barn and kennels. Then we'll come back and have a nice, relaxing lunch."

"Okay," said Cassie. She grabbed a leash and clipped it to Coco's collar.

Shadow rubbed against Cassie's leg. "Mom, can Shadow come too?"

Mom smiled. "Of course. Sometimes I think she's more dog than cat."

Cassie put on Shadow's leash. Yes, Shadow has a special cat leash.

As Mom attached my leash, she gave my head a pat. "I was hoping we could take a long walk in the woods today, Dash, but things are busier than—"

Ding-dong!

Mom opened the door. It was Martha, the groomer.

"Hi, guys," said Martha. She quickly shut the door. "It sure is getting blustery out there."

"Hi, Martha," said Mom. "Cassie and I are just heading over to the barn and kennels." Mom held up the phone. "Better bring this with us," she said, and laughed. "It's been ringing all morning."

Ding-dong!

"That must be Monsieur Petit," said Martha.

Monsieur Petit is a miniature French poodle. He's been coming to Animal Inn for his weekly

grooming appointment ever since we opened.

But it was not Monsieur Petit. It was a Labradoodle badly in need of a bath.

"What's that smell?" asked Cassie. The unmistakable aroma of skunk blew into the Welcome Area.

"Can we help you?" Mom said to the dog's owner.

"I hope so," said the woman. She wore a big, floppy hat, which she held on to with one hand, to keep it from blowing away. "I'm Wilhelmina, and this is Felix," she said, stepping inside and closing the door. "Felix is a bit . . . *skunky*. So when I received your coupon for fifty percent off, I thought, *Perfect!* And we came right over."

"*Fifty* percent off?" asked Martha.

"Small typo," Mom said sheepishly.

"I can take him after Monsieur Petit," Martha offered.

"Thank you," Mom said with a sigh. She turned to Felix's owner. "This is Martha, our groomer. Why don't I bring Felix to the outdoor play area until Martha's ready for him?"

Ding-dong!

"*That* must be Monsieur Petit," said Martha. She opened the door.

This time it *was* Monsieur Petit.

"Ooh la la," he muttered under his breath. "Something here is smellier than a French cheese."

"Mmm, cheese," moaned Coco.

"It's this guy," whispered Shadow, pointing with her crinkled nose.

"Sorry," mumbled Felix, a bit embarrassed.

Mom held Felix's leash in one hand and the phone in the other. "Cassie, do you have everybody else?"

Cassie nodded, gathering leashes.

"Okay, crew," said Mom. "Let's cast off!"

"I'll be back soon!" called Monsieur Petit's owner, Madame Gigi.

"I'll be back soon!" called Felix's owner, Wilhelmina.

I looked at Leopold. "I'll be back soon," I whispered.

CHAPTER
8

"Whoa!" shouted Cassie. "It's

windy out here!"

She was having a hard time holding on to the

leashes and keeping her hair out of her eyes.

"You walk ahead," Mom called to Cassie. "You

don't want to be downwind of Felix."

Poor Felix. He had probably just wanted to

play with the skunk but had gotten a little too

close. Now you could smell him a mile away.

"Let me put Felix in the play area," said Mom. "The fresh air will do him good."

Afterward she slid open the heavy barn door. The wind rushed in, blowing bits of hay into tiny cyclones.

We all piled inside. Mom slid the large door closed. Cassie undid all of our leashes. Shadow scampered straight to the loft. Coco flopped onto a mound of hay. I stayed close to Mom.

The building had once been a cow barn, but today our only guest was a beige-colored alpaca named Dandelion. She was staying with us while her owners repaired her shelter at home.

Mom raked out Dandelion's stall. She gave her fresh water. Cassie brought over some hay.

"Sorry I haven't gotten you out to the pasture

today," Mom said to Dandelion. "It's been busier than I expected."

"I think Dandelion's happy in here," said Cassie, gently stroking her neck. "It's too windy out there."

"She's right," Dandelion whispered to me with a toothy smile. We could all hear the wind blowing.

Coco and I followed Mom and Cassie to the back of the barn. Mom opened the door to the kennels. Each dog gets a private enclosure with a door to an outside run. On nice days the dogs are free to go in and out whenever they choose.

I always enjoy visiting the kennels and meeting new guests. Our current guests included a hound named Houdini, a Portuguese water dog named Walter, and a Pomeranian puppy named Penny.

The cats have smaller enclosures, each with

its own window to see outside.

We had only one feline guest, a cuddly calico named Cassandra.

I could hear Penny, the puppy, quietly crying in her kennel.

"What's wrong?" I asked her.

"Are you hungry?" asked Coco.

"I'm scared," Penny whimpered. "Too many strange noises."

The wind whistled. A tree branch cracked nearby. I was little scared too, and the pirates hadn't even arrived yet.

"It's just the wind," I said, trying to comfort her.

"I want to go home," Penny said.

Mom gave the dogs fresh water. Cassie refilled their food bowls. Then Mom noticed Penny cowering in the corner.

"Oh, little one," she said. "Not the best weather for your first trip away from home."

Mom reached into Penny's kennel and picked her up. "Why don't you come back to the inn with us for a little bit?"

"Yay!" cheered Cassie. "Can I carry her?"

"Sure," said Mom.

Coco and I followed Mom and Cassie back into the barn.

"Shadow!" Cassie called. "It's time to go."

Ring-ring!

Ring-ring!

"Animal Inn," answered Mom.

Shadow appeared, her fur dotted with bits of hay. "Who's that in Cassie's arms?" she whispered to Coco and me.

"That's Penny," I said.

"She's a little nervous," said Coco.

"She should meet my brother," said Shadow.

Mom hung up the phone. "We'd better get back to the inn," she said to Cassie. "Our last-minute guests will be here momentarily. And I still don't know where to put that treasure."

CHAPTER
9

Back in the Welcome Area, Mom

and Cassie took off our leashes and hung them up.

"Let's find a comfy place for Penny on the third floor," Mom said to Cassie. "We can check on the upstairs guests, and then, I promise, we'll have lunch."

Cassie followed Mom upstairs, with Penny snuggled in her arms.

"Anything to report?" I asked Leopold.

"All quiet here," Leopold said. "Smooth sailing."

"Yes, very quiet," agreed Whiskers from the sofa. He stood up and stretched. "Monsieur Petit has already been picked up. Martha just brought Felix into the grooming room. He sure was stinky, but now I smell lavender. It's very relaxing. It might turn out to be a quiet day after all."

"Except—" I started.

"Except *what*?" Whiskers said with alarm.

"Except the pirates will be here any second," Shadow said with a grin.

"Why didn't anybody warn me?" asked Whiskers.

"We just found out ourselves," I said.

Whiskers gulped. "We need to do something."

"I'm too hungry to do anything," moaned Coco. "When's lunch?"

"Let's use the element of surprise," suggested Shadow. "When the pirates arrive, I'll leap out from behind the sofa and swipe at their ankles with a swish and a slash." Shadow made dramatic sword-fighting motions with her paws.

"Maybe I can speak with their parrot," said Leopold. "I always find talking to be the best strategy."

"I agree," I said. "We need to stay calm and—"

Whoosh!

The door blew open. The wind rushed in.

"Hit the deck!" cried Whiskers. "It's a raid!"

"It's just the wind," I said.

"Wait a minute," said Leopold. He flew over to the open door. Leaves and dust whipped and swirled outside. He slowly raised his head, trying to make out something in the distance.

"What are you looking at?" Whiskers asked nervously.

"It's hard to see, with the wind blowing leaves this way and that," Leopold said. "But I think there's a person coming up the driveway, walking strangely."

"Strangely?" asked Coco. "You mean like this?" Coco did a silly walk in front of the sofa.

"No," said Leopold. "The figure seems to be limping."

"Maybe it's a pirate with a peg leg," said Coco.

"There's only *one* pirate?" asked Shadow. "I can handle one pirate with my paws tied behind my back."

"Wait," said Leopold. "There are now two figures." He looked a little shaken.

"*Two* pirates?" shrieked Whiskers.

"The second one is carrying something heavy," added Leopold.

"I bet it's the treasure," said Shadow.

"Or a giant piece of cheese," said Coco.

"Hold on," said Leopold. He strained to see out the door. He held up a wing to protect his eyes from the wind. "I think I see a third figure."

"*Three* pirates?" squealed Whiskers. "Abandon ship!"

"Now, now," I said. "Let's steady ourselves."

"Or retreat," said Leopold. "The third one appears to have a sword."

CHAPTER
10

Whiskers let out an ear-piercing

yowl.

Shadow jumped behind the sofa.

Leopold retreated to his perch, and then raised one wing like a shield.

Coco pretended to be asleep.

I stood my ground, but I admit I closed my eyes. What would happen now? Would we have to walk the plank? Would we be buried with the treasure? Was this the end of Animal Inn?

The wind rushed in. I heard footsteps approaching. I slowly opened one eye. And there . . . in the doorway . . . stood . . .

Jake, Dad, and Ethan.

"Hi, guys," said Ethan.

"Why is the door open?" asked Dad.

Jake was standing on one leg, leaning on a walking stick. Dad carried a large duffel bag. Ethan held a tent pole like a sword.

Mom and Cassie rushed downstairs.

"What happened?" Mom asked, coming over to help them.

"Wind advisory," said Dad, shutting the door behind him. "We couldn't get the tent to stay up. Then Jake chased some napkins that went flying . . ."

"Tripped and twisted my ankle," Jake said with grimace.

"It was *so* windy," said Ethan, holding up the pole in his hand, "even the poles were blowing away."

"We could have used Coco and Dash," Dad said. "Lots of fetching to do. I think next time we'll find a campground that allows dogs."

Cassie smiled.

"Come on," said Mom. "We were just about to have lunch. I can whip up a few more grilled cheese sandwiches."

Coco stood up, bright-eyed and alert.

"Sounds great," said Dad. "We can unload the car later. I had to park down by the road. There's a fallen limb across the driveway."

"And let's get some ice on that ankle," Mom said to Jake.

They all went upstairs, Jake leaning on Dad and taking one stair at a time. Coco followed.

"I have to admit, I feel a little foolish," I said.

"Me too," said Leopold. "To think it was Dad and the boys the whole time."

"And not a band of pirates," said Whiskers. He laughed. "Leopold, you might want to get your eyes checked. Really? A peg leg and a sword?"

"Shhh!" whispered Shadow, popping out from behind the sofa. "Did you hear that?"

"Hear what?" asked Leopold.

Scritch-scritch!

Scritch-scritch!

"That!" said Shadow. She looked worried. And Shadow rarely looks worried.

"I think it's just the wind," I said.

"Now who's the scaredy-cat, Shadow?" said

Whiskers with a chuckle. He jumped down from the sofa and strutted over to the front door. "A few blustery pirates are no match for me."

Scritch-scritch!

Creeeeak!

The door opened a few inches. Leopold, Shadow, and I took a step back.

Whiskers bravely stood his ground. "It's just the wind," he said.

Whoooosh!

A sudden gust blew the door wide open. And there . . . in the doorway . . . we saw . . .

A tall figure wearing an eye-patch, with a parrot on its shoulder.

"Over here, Blackbeard!" the figure called. "This is the place!"

"YOWWWL!" Whiskers shrieked in fright. *"YOWWWL!"*

The pirate flinched. The parrot on its shoulder squawked in alarm, and then flew off into the gusty afternoon.

"Treasure!" shouted the figure, running after the bird. "Treasure! Come back!"

CHAPTER
11

"PI-RATE!" yelled Fuzzy, popping

out from the heating vent. He was completely out of breath.

"We spotted it from the crow's nest," added Furry, popping out next.

"You're a little late," said Shadow. "The pirate already abandoned ship. It took off after a parrot."

"I believe it was an African gray parrot," said Leopold.

"Whiskers scared it," said Shadow.

"I scared *it*?" Whiskers exclaimed. "It scared *me*."

"But where's the dog?" asked Fuzzy.

"What dog?" I asked.

"We definitely saw a pirate, a parrot, and a dog," added Furry.

Suddenly the pirate reappeared in the doorway. Whiskers's fur stood up on end. Fuzzy and Furry jumped back into the heating vent.

"Hello?" the pirate called into the Welcome Area. "Is anybody here? I need help!"

It didn't sound much like a pirate. It sounded more like a worried pet owner.

Mom and Dad rushed downstairs. Cassie and Coco followed.

"Can we help you?" asked Mom.

"I'm Annie," the woman said. "We spoke earlier. But I just lost Treasure!"

"Oh no," gasped Mom. She turned to Dad. "This is Annie Drake. Her pets are staying with us while she has eye surgery."

Cassie looked around. "But where's Blackbeard?" she asked.

"He's already looking for Treasure," said Annie. "Treasure was in her harness, but then the wind blew and a cat yowled. Somehow she broke free and flew away."

"We should spread out and circle the area," said Dad.

"Cassie, you stay here," said Mom. "Tell the boys we'll be back soon."

Cassie headed upstairs. Mom, Dad, and Annie rushed outside. They were in such a hurry that no one checked to make sure the door was completely shut.

"Whew," said Whiskers. "I'm glad they're not real pirates. Now we can relax."

"Not quite," I said. "We need to help find Treasure."

"You mean outside?" cried Whiskers. "I'm an indoor cat."

"I'll stay here with Whiskers in case Treasure comes back," said Leopold.

"What about us?" said Fuzzy, popping back out of the heating vent.

"We know kung fu," added Furry.

"I don't think kung fu will be necessary," I said. "You two head back to the crow's nest and keep watch. Coco, you cover the yard. Shadow, you're in charge of bushes and hedges. I'll take the barn and kennels. We're going on a Treasure hunt!"

CHAPTER
12

I nudged the front door open

with my nose. The wind whipped and the leaves

swirled. We braced ourselves and headed outside.

Coco searched the yard. "Treasure," she called.

"Where are you, Treasure?"

Shadow searched in the hedges. "Treasure," I

heard her call. "Are you in here, Treasure?"

I hurried off to the barn and kennels. I could

see Mom, Dad, and Annie down by the road, still looking. But there was no sign of Treasure.

The barn door was open a little. Maybe Treasure had flown inside to escape the wind.

"Hi, Dash," said Dandelion, the alpaca. "Back so soon?"

"What?" I asked.

"Well, you just ran through, of course," said Dandelion.

I was confused. "Dandelion, have you seen a gray parrot?"

"Silly, you just asked me that!" said Dandelion with her toothy grin.

I scratched at the kennel door. It was shut tight.

"Can you hear me?" I called to the guests inside. "It's me, Dash. Has anyone seen a gray parrot?"

"No," Houdini, the hound, called back.

"But we'll keep an eye out," called Walter, the Portuguese water dog.

"Wait!" It was Cassandra, the calico cat. "Someone just flew by my window."

I ran back outside. But the only thing I saw flying by Cassandra's window was a huge leaf caught in the wind.

I scanned the field and sniffed at the air. Nothing.

I looked back toward Animal Inn. Nothing.

I looked down the driveway. Mom and Annie were standing next to Annie's car. I saw Mom put an arm around Annie's shoulders to comfort her.

Then I had a frightening thought.

What if we *didn't* find Treasure? It would be dark before long. Treasure would be outside in the wind and the cold. All alone.

Shiver me timbers. Maybe we were sunk.

Feeling defeated, I started toward to the inn. I hadn't taken more than a few steps when I felt something on my neck, clinging to my collar.

"Was that a lion that yowled?" said a small voice next to my ear. "Or a tiger?"

"Um—" I started.

"Whatever it was, it was scary," said the voice. "Right, Blackbeard?"

"Oh, my name's not—" I stopped talking. But I kept walking.

"I'm glad I found you, Blackbeard," said the voice. "I was so scared. And I don't want Annie to leave. And it's so windy today. And there was that lion noise. And my harness was loose. And then I got lost."

No doubt about it. I had found Treasure. Or rather, Treasure had found me.

She sighed. I could feel her body relax. I kept walking.

Then suddenly a dog came running across the field. It looked just like ... *me*! It was another Tibetan terrier. We were almost twins, except the fur on my chin is white, and the fur on its chin was black.

Now I understood. Black. Beard.

"Oh, hi, Blackbeard," said Treasure. Then I felt her suddenly stiffen. "Wait!" she said. "If you're Blackbeard ... who's *this*?"

Blackbeard smiled. "This is our lucky charm."

Treasure flew over to Blackbeard and looked back at me, a little confused.

"I'm Dash," I said. "Welcome to Animal Inn."

Blackbeard and I hit it off right away. Like I said, we Tibetan terriers make very good companions. Together we headed back to the inn. I could see

Fuzzy and Furry cheering from the crow's nest. Coco and Shadow met us at the front door.

Mom, Dad, and Annie came running up the driveway.

"Treasure!" said Annie. "My precious Treasure." She gently took Treasure from Blackbeard.

"Dash? Coco? Shadow?" Mom asked. "How did you three get out?"

"I guess all's well that ends well," said Dad.

We went inside to the Welcome Area. Whiskers was in his usual spot on the sofa. Leopold was on his perch. Jake, Ethan, and Cassie were downstairs too. Mom introduced everyone. Annie told the Tylers a little bit about herself and her pets.

"I'll be back in a few days to pick you up," Annie assured Blackbeard and Treasure. Mom and Dad walked Annie out to her car.

"Wow," said Jake. "Annie has the coolest job."

"I know," said Ethan.

"When I grow up," said Cassie, "I want to be a harbor pirate just like Annie."

"Cassie, it's harbor *pilot*. Not harbor *pirate*," corrected Ethan.

"That's what I said," insisted Cassie. "Harbor pirate." She tried hard to make the *L* sound, but it still came out like "pirate."

"Annie helps to guide ships, not raid and rob them," said Jake.

"Plus, why would a pirate ever come to Animal Inn?" said Ethan.

"Yeah, that would be ridiculous," said Cassie.

I looked at Leopold. Leopold looked at me.

Yes. Totally ridiculous.

EPILOGUE

I learned a lot of important

lessons from our pirate scare:

1. Wearing an eye-patch and owning a parrot do not necessarily make you a pirate.

2. Treasures come in all shapes and sizes.

3. A fifty-percent-off coupon can be very good for business.

4. Sooner or later crows will come back to roost.

(And they don't mind gerbils so much.)

By Sunday morning Animal Inn was like a calm sea. The sky was blue. The wind had disappeared. It was a perfect day.

Mom took Blackbeard and me on a long walk in the woods.

Jake's ankle felt better after he had a good night's sleep.

Ethan told Leopold all about the camping adventure.

And Cassie found the perfect place to keep Annie's Treasure—*in her room.*

"Penny, Treasure, and I slept very well last night," said Cassie.

"But I put Penny on the third floor," said Mom.

"Well . . . ," said Cassie with a smile.

Dad came in from clearing the tree limb that had been blocking the driveway.

"I might need glasses," he said.

"Why?" asked Mom.

"I'm positive I just saw Fuzzy and Furry on the roof," said Dad, scratching his head. "It looked like they were having a conversation with some crows."

"That's impossible," said Ethan.

"They're in the gerbiltorium," said Jake.

"Are you sure?" asked Mom.

Ethan rushed upstairs to check. Jake limped close behind.

Ding-dong!

"That's probably another customer with a coupon," said Mom, sighing.

"You relax," said Dad. "I'll get it."

But it wasn't a customer. It was a delivery person.

"Special delivery," she said.

Dad took the package and thanked her. He turned to Mom, a bit puzzled. "I didn't order anything. Did you?"

"Not me," said Mom. "Who's it from?"

Dad looked at the mailing label. "Picture *Purr*fect?" he said.

"Can I open it?" begged Cassie. *"Please."*

Cassie opened the box. Packing peanuts tumbled onto the floor.

"It's a photo!" said Cassie. She held it up for Mom and Dad to see. "It's so cute."

Mom and Dad sure looked confused.

"I didn't order it," said Mom.

"Me either," said Dad.

"We can hang it in the office," Cassie said excitedly.

"I guess I'll get the hammer," said Dad.

"I'll get a picture hook," said Mom. "But who would send us a framed photo of Fuzzy and Furry?"

I looked at Leopold. Leopold looked at me.

Those little scallywags.

FIND OUT WHAT HAPPENS IN THE NEXT **ANIMAL INN** STORY.

Beep-beep!

Beep-beep!

Yippee! The school bus is here.

Beep-beep!

Welcome to Animal Inn. My name is Coco. I'm a chocolate Labrador retriever.

No, I'm not made of chocolate, silly. I don't even like the stuff. We dogs aren't supposed to eat chocolate. But I do like to eat. Especially cheese.

I like cheddar cheese and Swiss cheese and American cheese. I like cheese sticks and cheese balls and cheese puffs. I like mac-and-cheese and grilled cheese and cheese pizza.

Luckily, my human sister, Cassie, likes cheese as much as I do. Cassie and I belong to the Tyler family. Our family includes five humans—Mom, Dad, Jake, Ethan, and Cassie—and seven pets:

- Me
- Dash—a Tibetan terrier
- Leopold—a scarlet macaw
- Shadow and Whiskers—sister and brother cats
- and Fuzzy and Furry—a pair of very adventur-ous gerbils

The Tylers used to live in an apartment in the city. Back then, Mom and Dad had two children, Jake and Ethan, and two pets, Dash and Leopold. But when Cassie and I came along, Mom and Dad bought this old house in the country.

Animal Inn is one part hotel, one part school, and one part spa. As our brochure says, *We promise to love your pet as much as you do.*

Beep-beep!

Where are Jake, Ethan, and Cassie? It's time for them to go to school.

Before long, customers will start to arrive. On some days, there is so much coming and going, Animal Inn could use a revolving door. We might have a Pekinese here for a pedicure. A Siamese for a short stay. Or a llama for a long stay.

On the first floor, we have the Welcome Area,

the office, the classroom, the grooming room, and my favorite—the party and play room.

Our family lives on the second floor. This includes Fuzzy and Furry snug in their gerbil-torium in Jake and Ethan's room.

The third floor is for smaller guests. We have a Reptile Room, a Rodent Room, and a Small Mammal Room. Larger guests stay out in the barn and kennels.

Beep-beep!

Where are those kids?

What if they miss the bus? What if they miss school?

School is so awesome. There's story time and lunchtime and playtime. Not too long ago, I got to spend an entire day with Cassie's first-grade class. Let me tell you what happened. . . .

CHAPTER
1

It began like any other Monday.

When Cassie and I came downstairs that morning, Leopold was already on his perch. Dash sat nearby. Whiskers was curled up on the sofa, while Shadow hid behind it. (She likes to sneak outside whenever she gets the chance.)

Cassie chattered to me as usual. "My school job this week is snack helper," she said. She unzipped her backpack and pulled out her lunchbox. "Sit please, Princess Coco."

I sat. Cassie opened her lunchbox and took out a little snack-pack filled with cubes of cheese. She gave one to me.

Yum. Cheddar.

"Now, if you have a question," Cassie said to me, "you need to raise your paw." She held up another piece of cheese. "Show me your paw, please."

I raised my paw.

"Very good, Princess Coco. But I won't be able to call you 'Princess,'" she said sadly. "In first grade, make-believe is only for recess and choice time. So in class, I will just call you Coco."

Cassie backed up a few steps and patted her thighs. "Come, Coco," she called.

I trotted over and nudged her hand with my nose. She gave me another piece of cheese.

"Now for the fun part," Cassie said. She went to the supply closet and found her old backpack from preschool—the one that looks like a ladybug. I'd worn Cassie's ladybug backpack before, like the time we ran away to the barn.

Dash looked at Leopold. Leopold looked at Dash. Whiskers looked a little nervous. But I was curious. What was Cassie up to now?

"Sit please, Princess Coco. I mean, just Coco."

I sat.

"Show me your paw, Coco."

I raised a paw. Cassie held it in her hand. She gently guided my paw through the shoulder strap of the backpack. Then she guided my other paw through the other strap. The backpack was a little wobbly, so Cassie tightened it up.

"Cassie!" Mom called from upstairs. "Did you remember to brush your teeth?"

"Oops," Cassie said. "I'll be right back," she whispered to me. "You stay here." She tossed me another cube of cheese. She put the snack-pack back into her lunchbox and set it next to the sofa. Then she ran up the stairs.

I plopped down on the floor. Whew! That was a lot of activity for so early in the morning.

Shadow came out from her hiding spot behind the sofa. "What's with the ladybug?" she asked me. "Are you and Cassie running away again?"

"Don't be silly," I said. "It's a school day."

"Then why are you wearing a backpack?" asked Whiskers.

"Cassie put it there," I said.

"We know that," said Shadow. "But *why*?"

"It appears Cassie is bringing Coco to school today," said Dash.

"I agree," said Leopold. "Weekly job assignment. Question protocol. Make-believe-play rules."

"Well, I'm glad *I'm* not the one going to school," said Whiskers.

"I am not going to school," I said. I stretched out in my sunny spot. "I am going to take a nap."

Looking for another great book?
Find it
IN THE MIDDLE.

Fun, fantastic books for kids
in the in-be**TWEEN** age.

IntheMiddleBooks.com

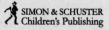

Did you LOVE reading this book?

Visit the Whyville...

Where you can:

- ○ Discover great books!
- ○ Meet new friends!
- ○ Read exclusive sneak peeks and more!

Log on to visit now!
bookhive.whyville.net

What happens when a bunch
of kids take over a forgotten
little garden plot?

the
FRIENDSHIP
garden